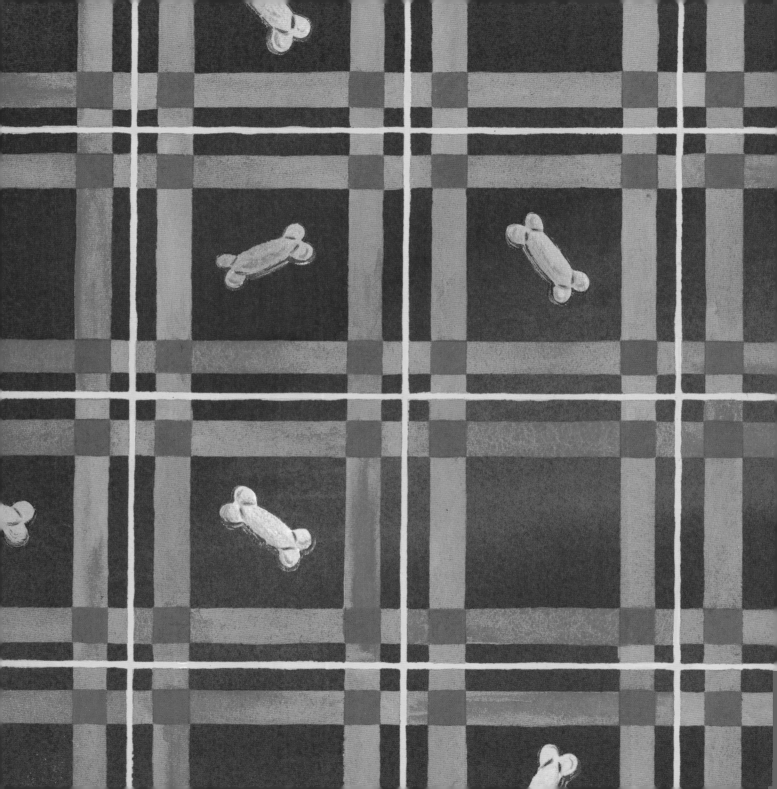

Merry Christmas, from Biscuit

story by ALYSSA SATIN CAPUCILLI
pictures by PAT SCHORIES

HarperFestival®
A Division of HarperCollins*Publishers*

"Guess what time it is, Biscuit!" said the little girl.

Woof, woof!

"It's time to celebrate Christmas once again!"

Woof!

"Come along, Biscuit. We need to finish our present for Grandma and Grandpa."

Woof, woof!

"I hope they like this Christmas album we're making for them."

Woof!

"Hold still, Biscuit!
A picture of you in front
of the Christmas tree is
just what we need."

Woof, woof!

Silly puppy! That candy cane belongs on the tree! Woof!

"Tonight, we'll sing Christmas carols."

Woof, woof!

"Let's take a picture by the piano."

Woof!

Oh, Biscuit! I can hardly wait to sing carols, too. Woof!

"Here are the stockings, hung by the chimney with care."
Woof, woof!

Oh, no! How did you get that stocking? Woof!

"We need to leave gingerbread and milk for Santa Claus."
Woof, woof!

Funny puppy! That gingerbread is for Santa! Woof!

Ding dong!

"There's the door, Biscuit!
Let's go!"

Woof, woof!

"Merry Christmas, Grandma and Grandpa!"

Woof!

"From both of us!"

"There's nothing better than celebrating Christmas with our family, our friends, and a silly little puppy like you, Biscuit!"

Woof, woof!

"Smile, Biscuit! Merry Christmas!"

Woof!

Merry Christmas! Woof!

Woof, woof!

Now it's your turn!
Have lots of fun making your own
Christmas album, just like Biscuit.
Merry Christmas.
Woof, woof!

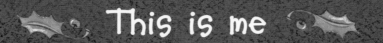

This is me

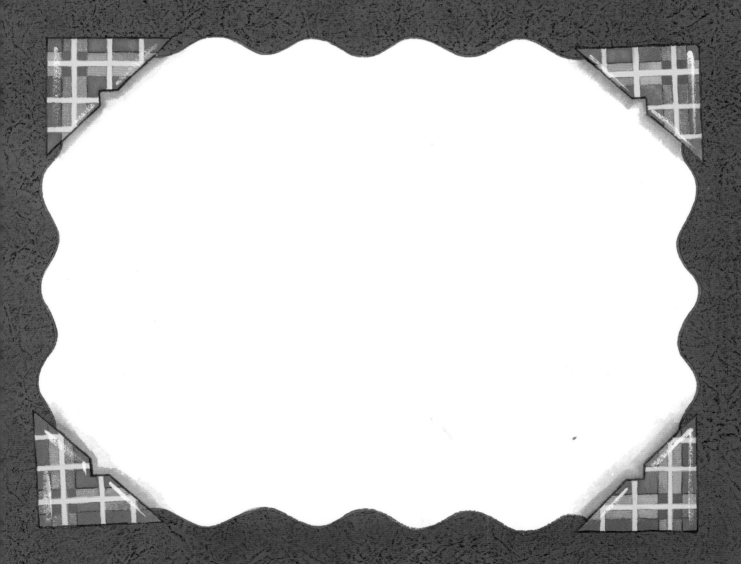

My Family Celebration

My Christmas Tree

My Christmas Wishes

My Christmas Favorites